# The Red Woollen
# Blanket

# Bob Graham

WALKER BOOKS
AND SUBSIDIARIES
LONDON · BOSTON · SYDNEY

Julia had her own blanket right from the start.

Julia was born in the winter. She slept in her special cot wrapped tight as a parcel.
She had a band of plastic on her wrist with her name on it.

"She's as bald as an egg," said her father,
helping himself to another chocolate.

Julia came home from the hospital with her new red blanket,
a bear, a grey woollen dog and a plastic duck.

Waiting at home for her were...

a large pair of pants with pink flowers and a beautiful blue jacket specially knitted by her grandmother.

"Isn't blue for boys?"
"No, it doesn't really matter," said Mum.

Wrapped up in the red woollen blanket, Julia
slept in her own basket...

or in the front garden in the watery winter sunshine.

Her hair sprouted from the holes in her tea-cosy hat.
She smiled – nothing worried Julia:

Julia grew. She slept in a cot and sucked and chewed the corners of her not-so-new blanket.

She rubbed the red woollen blanket gently against her nose.

Julia's mum carried her to the shops in a pack on
her back. The pack was meant to carry the shopping.

Julia liked it so much up there that the pushchair was
used for the shopping and the pack was used for Julia.

Then Julia was crawling and her blanket went with her.

It was chewed...

and screwed...

and oiled.

Some of it was left behind,

some went up the vacuum cleaner,

and some of it was trodden underfoot.

Then Julia took her first step.

Julia made her own small room from the blanket.
It was pink twilight under there.

From outside, the "creature" had a mind of its own.
It heaved and throbbed.

Wherever Julia went her blanket went too.

In the spring,

the summer,

the autumn,

and the winter.

Julia was getting bigger. Her blanket was getting smaller.
A sizeable piece was lost under the lawnmower.

"If Julia ran off deep into a forest," said her father, "she could find her way back by the blanket threads left behind."

The day that Julia started school,

she had a handy little blanket not much bigger than
a postage stamp –

because it would never do to take a whole blanket to school...

unless you were Billy, who used his blanket
as a "Lone Avenger's" cape.

Sometime during Julia's first day at school, she lost the last threads of her blanket.

It may have been while playing in the school yard...

or having her lunch under the trees.

It could have been anywhere at all…

and she hardly missed it.

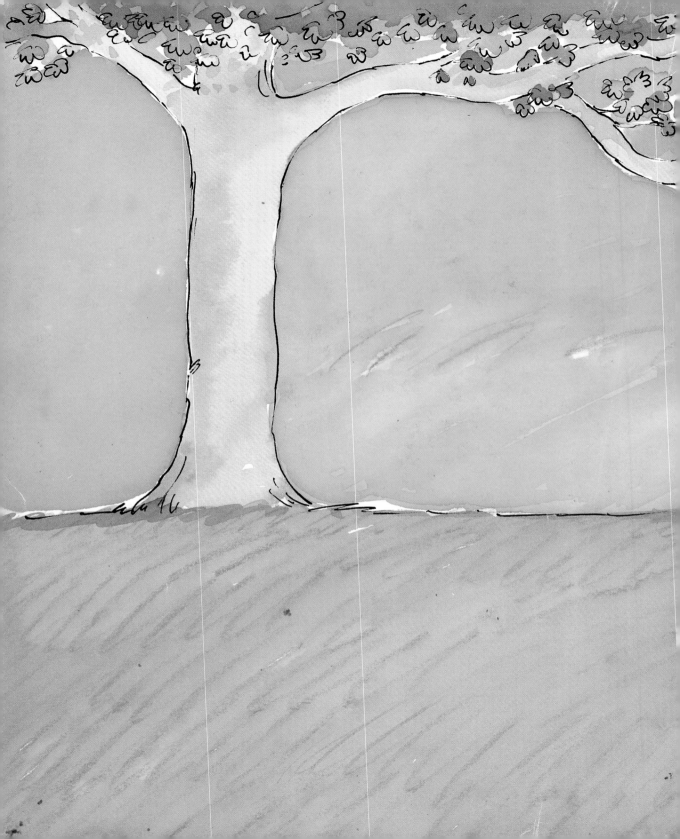